This book belongs to:

_____

Contents

Quick as a flash   3

Another dog's bone   11

Stargazers   15

Information pullout

New words   33

Learning to read
with this book   35

Read with Ladybird   36

Cover illustration by Trevor Parkin

Published by Ladybird Books Ltd
80 Strand London WC2R 0RL
A Penguin Company

8 10 9 7

© LADYBIRD BOOKS LTD MCMXCVII, MMI

LADYBIRD and the device of a Ladybird are trademarks of Ladybird Books Ltd

ISBN-13: 978-0-72142-394-4
Printed in China

milky swan
millions than
minutes throne
mountains together
names usual
queen worse
ready
remember
roared
shining
shooting
silly
sounds
star
story

Quick as
a flash

written by Marie Birkinshaw
illustrated by Jacqueline East

Anna's dad was always in a hurry,
and he hated to be kept waiting.

One morning, he was waiting
to take Anna to school as usual.
He called crossly upstairs,
"Anna! Are you coming?
I'm ready to go now."

"Yes!" Anna shouted.
"But I need a drink of water first."

"Well, come down and get one,"
said Dad. "Be as quick as a flash."

"I wish you wouldn't say that!" said Anna, when they were in the car.

"Say what?" asked Dad.

"Quick as a flash!" said Anna. "It sounds silly."

Dad just smiled.

The next day, Dad was waiting
to take Anna swimming.

"Time to go, Anna!" he said.

"But I'm not ready!" she cried.

"Well, hurry up and get ready!"
Dad called. Then he smiled
and said, "Quick as a flash!"

Anna groaned and covered her ears
with her hands.

A few days later, Dad was busy fixing a light bulb. This time Anna was waiting for him to take her to a dancing class.

"Hurry up, Dad!" said Anna.

"I'm coming," said Dad.

Quick as a...

"Well, I won't say that again!"
said Dad.

Another dog's bone

One of Aesop's fables
illustrated by Jackie Morris

One day, a hungry dog took
a bone from a shop.
He ran off with it before anyone
could stop him.

Soon he came
to a river.
He looked in it
and saw another dog
in the water.

"That dog's bone looks much
juicier than mine!" thought
the hungry dog. "I'll jump in
and take it from him."

So he jumped in.
At once, the other dog
and its bone disappeared.

To make things worse, the hungry dog had also lost his own bone in the water.

He walked sadly away to look for another bone.

Moral: Beware of being greedy!

Stargazers

written by Marie Birkinshaw
illustrated by Trevor Parkin

Grandad took Sally and Tom
to see the night sky.

"Tell us a story about the stars,"
said Tom.

"All right," said Grandad.
"Here's a story that helps me
to remember their names."

Once upon a time, there was
a beautiful queen who sat on
a golden throne.
She loved to look down at
the beautiful Earth below.

An enormous dragon was
jealous of the Queen's beauty.
He called for a big black cloud
to cover the Earth. This made
the Queen very sad.

The other stars loved the Queen
and wanted to help her. So that
night, a silver swan came
swimming through the cloud
and showed the Queen
all the shining seas
and rivers below.

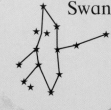

Swan

The dragon was angry and called for more clouds.

The next night, a giant lion leapt
through the clouds. He showed
the Queen all the amazing animals
on the Earth below.

Lion

Now the dragon became really
angry and called for more and
more clouds.
"Your friends will never get
through this," he roared.

But that night, two bears – a big bear and a little bear – raced through the clouds. They showed the Queen all the Earth's beautiful mountains. And soon she was happy again.

Great Bear and Little Bear

This time the dragon became
so angry and so jealous of the
Queen that he pushed her into
a big black hole and roared,
"Now you'll never see anything
ever again!"

The other stars saw what the
dragon had done.
They asked for help from the stars
at the other side of the Earth.
Together they pulled and pulled
until the Queen came out of
the big black hole...

and then together they pushed
the big bad dragon in!

"And, you know," said Grandad, "the Queen never saw that dragon again!"

"That was a lovely story," Sally said.

"Grandad, what's a shooting star?" asked Tom.

"I don't know," said Grandad. "Let's go inside and look it up in a book!"

Some stars of the northern sky

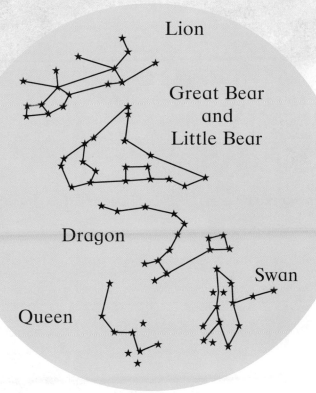

Lion

Great Bear
and
Little Bear

Dragon

Queen

Swan

Some stars of the southern sky

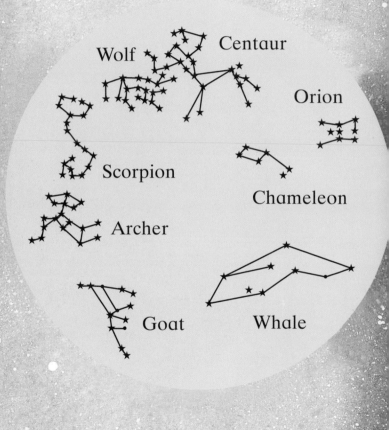

Did you know that?

⭐ Every star is a sun – an enormous ball of very hot gas.

⭐ The stars are millions and millions of kilometres away from Earth.
Our Sun is 150 million kilometres away.

⭐ Light from our Sun takes more than eight minutes to reach Earth.

⭐ Bunches of stars are called star clusters. One of the biggest star clusters is called The Milky Way.

When stars are new they are really hot. Really hot stars are so bright and white that they can look blue. As stars get older, they get colder and turn red.

Shooting stars are not stars at all – they are small bits of dust that burn up as they get nearer the Earth.

Learning to read with this book

Special features

Stargazers and other stories is ideal for early independent reading. It includes:

• two long stories to build stamina.

• interesting facts for your child to read for herself.

Planned to help your child to develop her reading by:

• practising a variety of reading techniques such as recognising frequently used words on sight, being able to read words with similar spelling patterns (eg, look/book), and the use of letter-sound clues.

• using rhyme to improve memory.

• including illustrations that make reading even more enjoyable.

Read with Ladybird

Read with Ladybird has been written to help you to help your child:

- to take the first steps in reading
- to improve early reading progress
- to gain confidence

Main Features

- **Several stories and rhymes in each book**

This means that there is not too much for you and your child to read in one go.

- **Rhyme and rhythm**

Read with Ladybird uses rhymes or stories with a rhythm to help your child to predict and memorise new words.

- **Gradual introduction and repetition of key words**

Read with Ladybird introduces and repeats the 100 most frequently used words in the English language.

- **Compatible with school reading schemes**

The key words that your child will learn are compatible with the word lists that are used in schools. This means that you can be confident that practising at home will support work done at school.

- **Information pullout**

Use this pullout to understand more about how you can use each story to help your child to learn to read.

But the most important feature of **Read with Ladybird** is for you and your child to have fun sharing the stories and rhymes with each other.